THE
GRAVEYARD
BOOK Volume 2

THE GRAVEYARD BOOK VOLUME 2

Based on the novel by: NEIL GAIMAN

Adapted by: P. CRAIG RUSSELL

Illustrated by: DAVID LAFUENTE SCOTT HAMPTON
P. CRAIG RUSSELL KEVIN NOWLAN GALEN SHOWMAN

Colorist: LOVERN KINDZIERSKI

Letterer: RICK PARKER

BLOOMSBURY
LONDON · NEW DELHI · NEW YORK · SYDNEY

Bloomsbury Publishing, London, New Delhi, New York and Sydney

First published in Great Britain in September 2014 by Bloomsbury Publishing Plc
50 Bedford Square, London WC1B 3DP

Published by arrangement with HarperCollins Children's Books,
a division of HarperCollins Publishers, 195 Broadway, New York, NY 10007

www.bloomsbury.com

Bloomsbury is a registered trademark of Bloomsbury Publishing Plc

Text copyright © 2008 by Neil Gaiman
Illustrations copyright © 2014 by P. Craig Russell

A CIP catalogue record for this book is available from the British Library

ISBN 978 1 4088 5900 1

Lettering by Rick Parker
Typography by Brian Durniak
Printed in China by C&C Offset Printing Co Ltd, Shenzhen, Guangdong

1 3 5 7 9 10 8 6 4 2

To Brooke and Andrew, Jadon and Josiah, and Naomi and Emmeline
(and special thanks to Galen Showman and Scott Hampton for service above and beyond)
—P.C.R.

6
Nobody Owens' School Days

Illustrated by David Lafuente

RAIN IN THE GRAVEYARD, AND THE WORLD
PUDDLED INTO BLURRED REFLECTIONS. BOD
SAT, CONCEALED FROM ANYONE, LIVING OR DEAD,
WHO MIGHT COME LOOKING FOR HIM, UNDER
THE ARCH THAT SEPARATED THE EGYPTIAN
WALK AND THE NORTHWESTERN WILDERNESS
BEYOND IT FROM THE REST OF THE GRAVEYARD,
AND HE READ HIS BOOK.

DAMM'EE!
DAMM'EE, SIR, AND
BLAST YOUR EYES!

THACKERAY PORRINGER, (1720-1734, SON OF THE ABOVE) CAME STAMPING UP THE SLIPPERY PATH. HE WAS A BIG BOY— HE HAD BEEN FOURTEEN WHEN HE DIED, FOLLOWING HIS INITIATION AS AN APPRENTICE TO A MASTER HOUSE PAINTER.

WHEN I CATCH YOU— AND FIND YOU, I SHALL— I SHALL MAKE YOU RUE THE DAY YOU WERE BORN.

≹SIGH≹

HE HAD BEEN GIVEN EIGHT COPPER PENNIES AND TOLD NOT TO COME BACK WITHOUT A HALF-A-GALLON OF RED AND WHITE STRIPED PAINT FOR PAINTING BARBER'S POLES.

THACKERAY HAD SPENT FIVE HOURS BEING SENT ALL OVER TOWN ONE SLUSHY JANUARY MORNING, BEING LAUGHED AT IN EACH ESTABLISHMENT HE VISITED AND THEN SENT ON TO THE NEXT.

WHEN HE REALIZED HE HAD BEEN MADE A FOOL OF, HE HAD TAKEN AN ANGRY CASE OF APOPLEXY, WHICH CARRIED HIM OFF WITHIN THE WEEK.

HE DIED GLARING FURIOUSLY AT THE OTHER APPRENTICES AND EVEN AT MR. HORROBIN, THE MASTER PAINTER.

I SCARCELY SEE WHAT ALL THE FUSS IS ABOUT. I UNDERWENT SO MUCH WORSE BACK WHEN I WAS A 'PRENTICE.

SO THACKERAY PORRINGER WAS BURIED WITH HIS COPY OF ROBINSON CRUSOE, WHICH WAS ALL THAT HE OWNED.

ROBINSON CRUSOE

DEATH HAD NOT IMPROVED THACKERAY PORRINGER'S TEMPER.

I KNOW YOU'RE HERE SOMEWHERE! COME OUT AND TAKE YOUR PUNISHMENT, YOU, YOU THIEF!

I'M NOT A THIEF, THACKERAY. I'M ONLY BORROWING IT. I PROMISE I'LL GIVE THE BOOK BACK WHEN I'VE FINISHED IT.

I TOLD YOU NOT TO!

BUT THERE ARE SO FEW BOOKS HERE. IT'S JUST UP TO A GOOD BIT, ANYWAY. HE'S FOUND A FOOTPRINT. IT'S NOT HIS. THAT MEANS SOMEONE ELSE IS ON THE ISLAND!

IT'S MY BOOK. GIVE IT BACK!

HERE.

I COULD READ IT TO YOU. I COULD DO THAT.

GO AND BOIL YOUR FAT HEAD!

OW!

OW!!

⚡#!

... 3 ...

AH!

OW!

OH .... HULLO

MISS EUPHEMIA HORSFALL AND TOM SANDS HAD BEEN STEPPING OUT TOGETHER FOR MANY YEARS. TOM HAD DIED DURING THE HUNDRED YEARS WAR WITH FRANCE, WHILE MISS EUPHEMIA (1861-1883, SHE SLEEPS, AYE, YET SHE SLEEPS WITH ANGELS) HAD BEEN BURIED IN VICTORIAN TIMES. THE COUPLE SEEMED TO HAVE NO TROUBLES WITH THE DIFFERENCES IN THEIR HISTORICAL PERIODS.

YOU SHOULD SLOW DOWN, YOUNG BOD. YOU'LL DO YOUR-SELF AN INJURY.

YOU ALREADY DID. YOUR MOTHER WILL HAVE WORDS WITH YOU.

AND YOUR GUARDIAN WAS LOOKING FOR YOU.

BUT IT'S STILL DAYLIGHT.

HE'S UP BETIMES AND SAID TO TELL YOU HE WANTED YOU. IF WE SAW YOU.

THANK YOU.

THE CHAPEL DOOR WAS OPEN, AND SILAS, WHO HAD LOVE FOR NEITHER THE RAIN NOR THE REMNANTS OF THE DAYLIGHT, WAS STANDING INSIDE.

I HEARD YOU WERE LOOKING FOR ME.

... 5 ...

... 7 ...

WHICH MEANS YOU'RE ASKING THE WRONG QUESTION.

HOW SO?

IF I GO OUTSIDE IN THE WORLD, THE QUESTION ISN'T "WHO WILL KEEP ME SAFE FROM HIM?"

NO?

NO. IT'S "WHO WILL KEEP HIM SAFE FROM ME?"

THE RAIN WAS DONE AND THE CLOUDY GLOAMING HAD BECOME TRUE TWILIGHT.

WE WILL NEED TO FIND YOU A SCHOOL.

NO ONE NOTICED THE BOY, NOT AT FIRST. NO ONE EVEN NOTICED THAT THEY HADN'T NOTICED HIM.

HE SAT HALFWAY BACK IN CLASS. HE DIDN'T ANSWER MUCH, NOT UNLESS HE WAS DIRECTLY ASKED A QUESTION, AND EVEN THEN HIS ANSWERS WERE SHORT AND FORGETTABLE, COLORLESS.

HE FADED, IN MIND AND IN MEMORY.

TEACHERS' STAFF ROOM

DO YOU THINK THEY'RE RELIGIOUS, HIS FAMILY?

WHOSE FAMILY?

OWENS IN EIGHT B.

THE TALL SPOTTY LAD?

I DON'T THINK SO. SORT OF MEDIUM HEIGHT.

WHAT ABOUT HIM?

HANDWRITES EVERYTHING. LOVELY HANDWRITING. WHAT THEY USED TO CALL COPPERPLATE.

AND THAT MAKES HIM RELIGIOUS BECAUSE...?

HE SAYS THEY DON'T HAVE A COMPUTER.

HE DOESN'T HAVE A PHONE.

AND?

I DON'T SEE WHY THAT MAKES HIM RELIGIOUS.

... 9 ...

HE'S A SMART LAD. THERE'S JUST STUFF HE DOESN'T KNOW. AND IN HISTORY, HE'LL THROW IN LITTLE MADE-UP DETAILS, STUFF NOT IN THE BOOKS.

WHAT KIND OF STUFF?

MR. KIRBY FINISHED MARKING BOD'S ESSAY. WITHOUT SOMETHING IMMEDIATELY IN FRONT OF HIM, THE WHOLE MATTER SEEMED UNIMPORTANT.

STUFF.

AND HE FORGOT ABOUT IT.

JUST AS HE FORGOT TO ENTER BOD'S NAME ON THE ROLL. JUST AS BOD'S NAME WAS NOT TO BE FOUND ON THE SCHOOL DATABASES.

STUDENTS

SCHOOL

SEARCH P

NO MATCHES

THE BOY WAS A MODEL PUPIL, FORGETTABLE, AND BASICALLY FORGOTTEN, AND HE SPENT MUCH OF HIS SPARE TIME IN THE SCHOOL LIBRARY, A LARGE ROOM FILLED WITH BOOKS AND OLD ARMCHAIRS, WHERE HE READ STORIES AS ENTHUSIASTIC- ALLY AS SOME CHILDREN ATE.

EVEN THE OTHER KIDS FORGOT ABOUT HIM. NOT WHEN HE WAS SITTING IN FRONT OF THEM: THEY REMEMBERED HIM THEN. BUT WHEN THAT OWENS KID WAS OUT OF SIGHT, HE WAS OUT-OF-MIND.

HIS PRESENCE WAS ALMOST GHOSTLY.

IT WAS DIFFERENT IF HE WAS THERE, OF COURSE.

... 10 ...

NICK FARTHING WAS TWELVE, BUT HE COULD PASS FOR SIXTEEN. HE WAS AN EFFICIENT SHOPLIFTER, AND OCCASIONAL THUG WHO DID NOT CARE ABOUT BEING LIKED, AS LONG AS THE OTHER KIDS, ALL SMALLER, DID WHAT HE SAID. ANYWAY, HE HAD A FRIEND. HER NAME WAS MAUREEN QUILLING.

CALL ME MO.

NICK LIKED TO SHOPLIFT, BUT MO TOLD HIM WHAT TO STEAL.

♪

NICK LIKED TO HURT AND INTIMIDATE, BUT MO POINTED HIM AT THE PEOPLE WHO NEEDED TO BE INTIMIDATED.

♪

THEY WERE, AS SHE TOLD HIM SOMETIMES...

A PERFECT TEAM.

THEY WERE SITTING IN A CORNER OF THE LIBRARY SPLITTING THEIR TAKE OF THE YEAR SEVENS' POCKET MONEY.

THE SINGH KID HASN'T COUGHED UP YET. YOU'LL HAVE TO FIND HIM.

YEAH. HE'LL PAY.

WHAT WAS IT HE NICKED? A CD?

YEH.

JUST POINT OUT THE ERROR OF HIS WAYS.

EASY.

WE'RE A GOOD TEAM.

LIKE BATMAN AND ROBIN.

MORE LIKE DOCTOR JEKYLL AND MISTER HYDE.

AND SOMEBODY WHO HAD BEEN READING, UNNOTICED, IN A WINDOW SEAT GOT UP AND WALKED OUT OF THE ROOM.

IS THAT WHAT NICK AND MO ARE WAITING FOR?

ARE YOU WITH THEM? NICK AND MO?

NOPE. I THINK THAT THEY ARE FAIRLY REPULSIVE.

ACTUALLY, I CAME TO GIVE YOU A BIT OF ADVICE.

YEAH?

DON'T PAY THEM.

EASY FOR YOU TO SAY.

BECAUSE THEY AREN'T BLACKMAILING ME?

THEY HIT YOU OR THREATENED YOU UNTIL YOU SHOPLIFTED A CD FOR THEM. THEN THEY TOLD YOU THAT UNLESS YOU HANDED OVER YOUR POCKET MONEY TO THEM, THEY'D TELL ON YOU. WHAT DID THEY DO, FILM YOU DOING IT?

YES.

THANK YOU. I HADN'T EVEN TRIED THE FEAR OUT ON LIVING PEOPLE. I MEAN, I KNEW THE THEORY, BUT. *WELL...*

THAT WAS GOOD, DEAR. A NICE FADE FIRST, THEN THE FEAR.

IT WORKED A TREAT. I'M AMABELLA PERSSON.

BOD. NOBODY OWENS.

THE *LIVE BOY?* FROM THE BIG GRAVE-YARD ON THE HILL? *REALLY?*

UM...

RODDY?

PORTUNA?

COME AND SEE WHO'S HERE!

MASTER OWENS, HERE WAS FRIGHTENING SOME CHILDREN WHO DOUBT-LESS DESERVED IT.

GOOD SHOW. BOUNDERS GUILTY OF REPREHENSIBLE BEHAVIOR, EH?

THEY WERE BULLIES. MAKING KIDS HAND OVER THEIR POCKET MONEY. STUFF LIKE THAT.

A FRIGHTENING IS CER-TAINLY A GOOD BEGINNING. AND WHAT HAVE YOU PLANNED IF IT DOES NOT WORK?

I HADN'T REALLY THOUGHT—

I SHOULD SUGGEST THAT DREAMWALKING MIGHT BE THE MOST EFFICIENT REMEDY. YOU *CAN* DREAMWALK, CAN YOU NOT?

I'M NOT SURE. MISTER PENNYWORTH SHOWED ME HOW, BUT I HAVEN'T REALLY— WELL, THERE'S SOME THINGS I ONLY REALLY KNOW IN THEORY...

GOING TO SCHOOL WITH THE LIVING DID NOT EXCUSE BOD FROM HIS LESSONS WITH THE DEAD. MR. PENNYWORTH HAD LITTLE TO COMPLAIN ABOUT THESE DAYS. BOD STUDIED HARD AND ASKED QUESTIONS. TONIGHT BOD ASKED ABOUT HAUNTINGS, GETTING MORE AND MORE SPECIFIC, EXASPERATING MR. PENNYWORTH, WHO HAD NEVER GONE IN FOR THAT SORT OF THING HIMSELF.

HOW *EXACTLY* DO I MAKE A COLD SPOT IN THE AIR?

I THINK I'VE GOT *FEAR* DOWN...

BUT HOW DO I TAKE IT UP ALL THE WAY TO TERROR?

WELL, UH...

SIGH, YOU...

OH, *HARRUMPH!*

MR. PENNYWORTH DID HIS BEST TO EXPLAIN, AND IT WAS GONE FOUR IN THE MORNING BEFORE THEY WERE DONE.

BOD WAS TIRED AT SCHOOL THE NEXT DAY. HE WAS DOING ALL HE COULD TO CONCENTRATE ON THE LESSON WHEN THERE WAS A KNOCK AT THE DOOR.

THE CLASS AND MR. KIRBY ALL LOOKED TO SEE WHO WAS THERE.

... 19 ...

MO QUILLING PASSED BOD IN THE CORRIDOR.

I'M NOT AFRAID OF YOU.

YOU'RE WEIRD. YOU DON'T HAVE ANY FRIENDS.

I DIDN'T COME HERE FOR FRIENDS. I CAME TO LEARN.

DO YOU KNOW HOW WEIRD THAT IS? NOBODY COMES TO SCHOOL TO *LEARN*. I MEAN, YOU COME BECAUSE YOU *HAVE* TO.

I'M NOT AFRAID OF YOU. WHATEVER TRICK YOU DID YESTERDAY, YOU DIDN'T SCARE *ME*.

OKAY.

BOD WONDERED IF HE HAD MADE A MISTAKE, GETTING INVOLVED. HE WAS BECOMING A PRESENCE, RATHER THAN AN ABSENCE. SILAS HAD WARNED HIM TO KEEP A LOW PROFILE, TOLD HIM TO GO THROUGH SCHOOL PARTLY FADED, BUT EVERYTHING WAS CHANGING.

··· 20 ···

... 21 ...

AND HE TURNED ON HIS
HEEL AND BEGAN TO WALK
DOWN THE PATH THAT LED
TO THE GATES AND OUT
OF THE GRAVEYARD.

SILAS WRAPPED THE SHADOWS AROUND HIM LIKE A BLANKET, AND STARED AFTER
THE WAY THE BOY HAD GONE, AND DID NOT MOVE TO FOLLOW.

NICK FARTHING WAS IN HIS BED, ASLEEP AND DREAMING OF PIRATES
ON THE SUNNY BLUE SEA, WHEN IT ALL WENT WRONG.

ONE MOMENT HE WAS THE CAPTAIN OF HIS OWN PIRATE SHIP — A HAPPY PLACE, CREWED BY OBEDIENT ELEVEN-YEAR-OLDS, EXCEPT FOR THE GIRLS, WHO WERE ALL A YEAR OR TWO OLDER THAN NICK.

AND THE NEXT...

AND THEN, IN THE WAY OF DREAMS, HE WAS STANDING ON THE BLACK DECK OF THE NEW SHIP.

YOU'RE NOT AFRAID OF ME.

DO YOU THINK YOU'RE A PIRATE, NICK?

YOU'RE THAT KID.

BOB OWENS.

... 24 ...

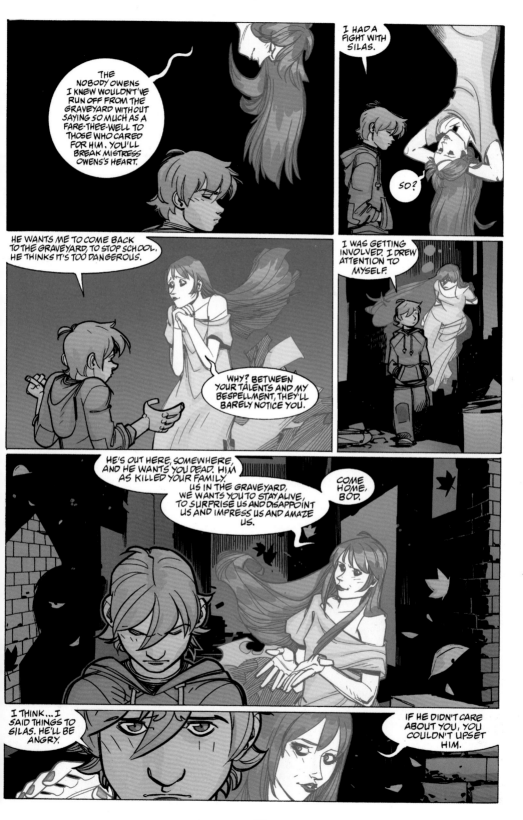

I SAW YOU FROM MY BEDROOM.

I THINK HE'S THE ONE WHO'S BEEN BREAKING WINDOWS.

WHAT'S YOUR NAME?

NOBODY.

OW!

DON'T GIVE ME THAT. JUST ANSWER THE QUESTIONS POLITELY. RIGHT?

BOD TRIED TO FADE, BUT FADING RELIES ON PEOPLE'S ATTENTION SLIDING AWAY FROM YOU, AND EVERYBODY'S ATTENTION WAS ON HIM THEN.

WHERE EXACTLY DO YOU LIVE?

YOU CAN'T ARREST ME FOR NOT TELLING YOU MY NAME OR ADDRESS.

NO, I CAN'T. BUT I *CAN* TAKE YOU DOWN TO THE STATION UNTIL YOU GIVE US THE NAME OF A RESPONSIBLE ADULT INTO WHOSE CARE WE CAN RELEASE YOU.

I SAW YOU FROM THE FRONT WINDOW, SO I CALLED THE POLICE.

I WASN'T *DOING* ANYTHING.

I WASN'T EVEN IN YOUR GARDEN. AND WHY ARE THEY BRINGING *YOU* OUT TO FIND ME?

QUIET BACK THERE!!!

WE'LL CALL YOU TOMORROW, LET YOUR MOM AND DAD KNOW WHAT WE FOUND.

THANKS, UNCLE TAM.

JUST DOING MY DUTY.

THEY DROVE BACK THROUGH THE TOWN IN SILENCE, BOD TRYING TO FADE AS BEST HE COULD, WITH NO SUCCESS. HE FELT SICK AND MISERABLE.

DO THEY HAVE *PRISONS* FOR KIDS?

IN ONE EVENING, I HAD MY FIRST REAL ARGUMENT WITH SILAS.

I TRIED TO RUN AWAY, FAILED, AND NOW I CAN'T GET BACK.

I CAN'T TELL THE POLICE MY NAME, OR WHERE I LIVE. I'LL SPEND THE REST OF MY LIFE IN A POLICE CELL, OR IN A PRISON FOR KIDS.

EXCUSE ME? DO THEY HAVE PRISONS FOR KIDS?

GETTING WORRIED, NOW, ARE YOU? I DON'T BLAME YOU. YOU KIDS. RUNNING WILD. SOME OF YOU NEED LOCKING UP, I'LL TELL YOU.

... 31 ...

YOU SHOULD THANK YOUR LITTLE WITCH-FRIEND. SHE CAME AND FOUND ME, TOLD ME YOU WERE IN TROUBLE, AND WHAT KIND OF TROUBLE YOU WERE IN.

WHAT HAPPENED TONIGHT WAS STUPID, WASN'T IT? I MEAN, I PUT THINGS AT RISK.

MORE THINGS THAN YOU KNOW, YOUNG NOBODY OWENS, YES.

YOU WERE RIGHT. I WON'T GO BACK, NOT TO THAT SCHOOL, AND NOT LIKE THAT.

MAUREEN QUILLING HAD HAD THE WORST WEEK OF HER LIFE.

NICK FARTHING WAS NO LONGER SPEAKING TO HER.

HER UNCLE TAM HAD SHOUTED AT HER ABOUT THE OWENS KID THING.

AND IF YOU *EVER* MENTION ANYTHING ABOUT THAT EVENING TO *ANYONE*, I COULD LOSE MY JOB AND I WOULDN'T WANT TO BE IN *YOUR* SHOES IF THAT HAPPENS.

EVEN THE YEAR SEVENS WEREN'T SCARED OF HER ANYMORE.

IT WAS ROTTEN.

SHE WANTED TO SEE THAT OWENS KID WRITHING IN MISERABLE AGONY. SHE WOULD CONCOCT ELABORATE REVENGE SCHEMES IN HER HEAD, COMPLEX AND VICIOUS. THEY WERE THE ONLY THING THAT MADE HER FEEL BETTER.

AND EVEN THEY DIDN'T REALLY HELP.

IF THERE WAS ONE JOB THAT GAVE MO THE CREEPS, IT WAS CLEANING UP THE SCIENCE LABS. IT STOOD TO REASON THAT HERE, IN THE WORST WEEK OF HER LIFE, IT WOULD BE HER TURN.

AT LEAST MRS. HAWKINS WAS THERE, COLLECTING PAPERS AT THE END OF THE DAY. HAVING HER THERE, HAVING ANYBODY THERE, WAS COMFORTING.

YOU'RE DOING A GOOD JOB, MAUREEN.

THANKS.

... 38 ...

... 39 ...

7
Every Man Jack

Illustrated by Scott Hampton

SILAS HAD BEEN PREOCCUPIED FOR THE PREVIOUS SEVERAL MONTHS. HE HAD BEGUN TO LEAVE THE GRAVEYARD FOR DAYS, SOMETIMES WEEKS, AT A TIME. OVER CHRISTMAS, MISS LUPESCU HAD COME OUT FOR THREE WEEKS IN HIS PLACE, AND BOD HAD SHARED HER MEALS IN HER LITTLE FLAT IN OLD TOWN. SHE HAD EVEN TAKEN HIM TO A FOOTBALL MATCH, AS SILAS HAD PROMISED THAT SHE WOULD, BUT SHE HAD GONE BACK TO THE PLACE SHE HAD CALLED "THE OLD COUNTRY" AFTER SQUEEZING HIS CHEEKS AND CALLING HIM HER PET NAME FOR HIM...

NIMENI.

NOW SILAS WAS GONE, AND MISS LUPESCU ALSO. MR. AND MRS. OWENS WERE SITTING OUTSIDE THE JOSIAH WORTHINGTON TOMB TALKING TO JOSIAH WORTHINGTON. NONE OF THEM WAS HAPPY.

YOU MEAN TO SAY THAT HE DID NOT TELL EITHER OF YOU *WHERE* HE WAS GOING OR HOW THE CHILD WAS TO BE CARED FOR?

NO!

WELL, WHERE *IS* HE?

HE'S NEVER BEEN GONE FOR SO LONG BEFORE. AND HE PROMISED, WHEN THE CHILD CAME TO US, HE WOULD BE HERE TO HELP US CARE FOR HIM. HE *PROMISED*.

I WORRY THAT SOMETHING MUST HAVE HAPPENED TO HIM.

THIS IS TOO BAD OF HIM! IS THERE NO WAY TO FIND HIM, TO CALL HIM BACK?

NONE THAT I KNOW. BUT I BELIEVE THAT HE'S LEFT MONEY IN THE CRYPT, FOR FOOD FOR THE BOY.

MONEY! WHAT USE IS *MONEY*?

BOD WILL BE NEEDING MONEY IF HE'S TO GO OUT THERE TO BUY FOOD.

YOU'RE ALL AS BAD AS EACH *OTHER*!

"MOSTLY, I HAD EYES FOR YOU. LET ME SEE... HE HAD DARK HAIR, VERY DARK. AND I WAS FRIGHTENED OF HIM. HE HAD A SHARP FACE. HUNGRY AND ANGRY, ALL AT ONCE, HE WAS. SILAS SAW HIM OFF."

WHY DIDN'T SILAS JUST KILL HIM? HE SHOULD HAVE JUST KILLED HIM THEN.

HE'S NOT A MONSTER, BOD.

IF SILAS HAD KILLED HIM BACK THEN, I WOULD BE SAFE NOW. I COULD GO ANYWHERE.

SILAS KNOWS MORE THAN YOU DO ABOUT ALL THIS. IT'S NOT THAT EASY.

WHAT WAS HIS NAME? THE MAN WHO KILLED THEM.

BUT YOU KNOW IT, DON'T YOU?

HE DIDN'T SAY IT. NOT THEN.

THERE'S NOTHING YOU CAN DO, BOD.

THERE IS. I CAN *LEARN*. I CAN LEARN *EVERYTHING* I NEED TO KNOW, ALL I CAN. I LEARNED ABOUT GHOUL-GATES. I LEARNED TO DREAMWALK. MISS LUPESCU TAUGHT ME HOW TO WATCH THE STARS. SILAS TAUGHT ME SILENCE. I CAN HAUNT. I CAN FADE. I KNOW EVERY *INCH* OF THIS GRAVEYARD.

≷SIGH≷

▼SILAS TOLD ME THE MAN WHO KILLED YOUR FAMILY WAS CALLED JACK. THAT'S ALL I KNOW.

MOTHER?

YES?

WHEN WILL SILAS COME BACK?

I WISH I KNEW.

... 47 ...

FRIGHT-FULLY SORRY.

I TOOK THE LIBERTY OF BRINGING YOUR DAUGHTER BACK TO YOU. OBVIOUSLY, YOU TAUGHT HER WELL, SHOULDN'T ACCEPT RIDES FROM STRANGERS.

BUT, WELL, IT WAS RAINING, SHE TOOK THE WRONG BUS, WOUND UP ON THE OTHER SIDE OF TOWN. BIT OF A MESS ALL AROUND, REALLY.

SAY YOU CAN FIND IT IN YOUR HEART TO FORGIVE. FORGIVE HER, AND, UM, ME.

WELL, YOU CAN'T BE TOO CAREFUL THESE DAYS. WOULD YOU LIKE A CUP OF TEA...

MISTER...?

FROST. BUT, PLEASE, CALL ME JAY.

CALL ME NOONA.

I'LL PUT THE KETTLE ON.

OVER TEA, SCARLETT TOLD HER MOTHER THE STORY OF HER WRONG BUS ADVENTURE, AND HOW SHE HAD FOUND HERSELF AT THE GRAVEYARD AND HOW SHE MET MR. FROST...

...BY THE LITTLE CHURCH.

CLINK

NOT QUITE WHAT I MEANT. HULLO. I'M BOD.

I'M SCARLETT.

OF COURSE, YOU ARE! I KNEW YOU LOOKED FAMILIAR. YOU WERE IN THE GRAVEYARD TODAY WITH THAT MAN, THE ONE WITH THE PAPER.

MR. FROST. HE'S REALLY NICE. DID YOU SEE US?

YEAH. I KEEP AN EYE ON MOST THINGS THAT HAPPEN IN THE GRAVEYARD.

WHAT KIND OF A NAME IS BOD?

IT'S SHORT FOR NOBODY.

OF COURSE. THAT'S WHAT THIS DREAM IS ABOUT. YOU'RE MY IMAGINARY FRIEND, FROM WHEN I WAS LITTLE. ALL GROWN UP.

YOU WERE REALLY BRAVE.

WE WENT DEEP INTO THE HILL AND WE SAW THE INDIGO MAN. AND WE MET THE SLEER.

SOMETHING HAPPENED THEN, IN HER HEAD. A RUSHING AND A TUMBLING, A WHIRL OF DARKNESS AND A CRASH OF IMAGES.

I REMEMBER.

BUT SHE SPOKE TO THE EMPTY DARKNESS OF HER BEDROOM, AND HEARD NOTHING IN REPLY BUT THE LOW TRUNDLE OF A DISTANT LORRY MAKING ITS WAY THROUGH THE NIGHT.

BOD HAD STORES OF FOOD, THE KIND THAT LASTED, CACHED IN THE CRYPT. HE HAD ENOUGH TO KEEP HIM GOING FOR A COUPLE OF MONTHS. SILAS HAD MADE SURE OF THAT.

BO'S

HE MISSED THE WORLD BEYOND THE GRAVEYARD GATES, BUT HE KNEW IT WAS NOT SAFE OUT THERE.

NOT YET.

THE GRAVEYARD, THOUGH, WAS HIS WORLD AND HIS DOMAIN, AND HE LOVED IT AS ONLY A FOURTEEN-YEAR-OLD BOY CAN LOVE ANYTHING.

AND YET...

IN THE GRAVEYARD, NO ONE EVER CHANGED. THE LITTLE CHILDREN BOD HAD PLAYED WITH WHEN HE WAS SMALL, WERE STILL LITTLE CHILDREN.

FORTINBRAS BARTLEBY, WHO HAD ONCE BEEN HIS BEST FRIEND, WAS NOW FOUR OR FIVE YEARS YOUNGER THAN BOD WAS, AND THEY HAD LESS TO TALK ABOUT EACH TIME THEY SAW EACH OTHER.

THACKERAY PORRINGER WAS BOD'S HEIGHT AND AGE, AND SEEMED TO BE IN MUCH BETTER TEMPER WITH HIM; HE WOULD WALK WITH BOD IN THE EVENINGS, AND TELL STORIES OF UNFORTUNATE THINGS THAT HAD HAPPENED TO HIS FRIENDS.

NORMALLY, THE STORIES WOULD END IN THE FRIENDS BEING HANGED UNTIL THEY WERE DEAD FOR NO OFFENSE OF THEIRS AND BY MISTAKE.

SOMETIMES THEY WERE SIMPLY TRANSPORTED TO THE AMERICAN COLONIES AND THEY DIDN'T HAVE TO BE HANGED UNLESS THEY CAME BACK.

LIZA HEMPSTOCK, WHO HAD BEEN BOD'S FRIEND FOR SIX YEARS, WAS DIFFERENT IN ANOTHER WAY.

BOD TALKED TO MR. OWENS ABOUT THIS.

IT'S JUST WOMEN, I RECKON.

SHE LIKED YOU AS A BOY. PROBABLY ISN'T SURE WHO YOU ARE NOW YOU'RE A YOUNG MAN.

I USED TO PLAY WITH ONE LITTLE GIRL DOWN BY THE DUCK-POND EVERY DAY UNTIL SHE TURNED ABOUT YOUR AGE, AND THEN SHE THREW AN APPLE AT MY HEAD AND DID NOT SAY ANOTHER WORD TO ME UNTIL I WAS SEVENTEEN.

!

IT WAS A *PEAR* I THREW.

AND I WAS TALKING TO YOU SOON ENOUGH, FOR WE DANCED A MEASURE AT YOUR COUSIN NED'S WEDDING, AND THAT WAS BUT TWO DAYS AFTER YOUR SIXTEENTH BIRTHDAY.

OF COURSE YOU ARE RIGHT, MY DEAR.

SEVENTEEN.

BOD HAD ALLOWED HIMSELF NO FRIENDS AMONG THE LIVING. THAT WAY LAY ONLY TROUBLE. STILL, HE HAD REMEMBERED SCARLETT, HAD MISSED HER FOR YEARS AFTER SHE WENT AWAY, HAD LONG AGO FACED THE FACT HE WOULD NEVER SEE HER AGAIN.

AND NOW SHE HAD BEEN HERE IN HIS GRAVE-YARD, AND HE HAD NOT KNOWN HER.

HE WAS WANDERING DEEPER INTO THE TANGLE OF IVY AND TREES THAT MADE THE NORTHWEST QUADRANT SO DANGEROUS. SIGNS ADVISED VISITORS TO KEEP OUT, BUT THE SIGNS WERE NOT NEEDED. NATURE HAD BEEN RECLAIMING THE GRAVEYARD FOR ALMOST A HUNDRED YEARS. PATHS WERE LOST AND IMPASSABLE.

WHEN BOD WAS NINE, HE HAD BEEN EXPLORING IN JUST THIS PART OF THE WORLD WHEN THE SOIL HAD GIVEN WAY BENEATH HIM, TUMBLING HIM INTO A HOLE ALMOST TWENTY FEET DOWN. THE GRAVE HAD BEEN DUG DEEP, TO ACCOMMODATE MANY COFFINS, BUT THERE WAS ONLY ONE COFFIN DOWN AT THE BOTTOM, CONTAINING A RATHER EXCITABLE MEDICAL GENTLE-MAN NAMED CARSTAIRS.

CARSTAIRS SEEMED THRILLED BY BOD'S ARRIVAL AND INSISTED ON EXAMINING BOD'S TWISTED FOOT.

ONLY THEN COULD HE BE PERSUADED TO GO AND FETCH HELP.

BOD WAS MAKING HIS WAY THROUGH THE NORTHWEST QUADRANT, A SLUDGE OF FALLEN LEAVES, A TANGLE OF IVY, WHERE THE FOXES MADE THEIR HOMES, BECAUSE HE HAD AN URGE TO TALK TO THE POET.

HERE LIES THE MORTAL REMAINS OF
NEHEMIAH TROT
POET
1741 – 1774
SWANS SING
BEFORE THEY DIE.

MIGHT I ASK FOR ADVICE?

OF COURSE, BRAVE BOY. THE ADVICE OF POETS IS THE CORDIALITY OF KINGS! HOW MAY I SMEAR UNCTION ON YOUR, NO, NOT UNCTION, HOW MAY I GIVE BALM TO YOUR PAIN?

I'M NOT ACTUALLY IN PAIN. I JUST—WELL, THERE'S A GIRL I USED TO KNOW, AND I WASN'T SURE IF I SHOULD FIND HER AND TALK TO HER OR IF I SHOULD JUST FORGET ABOUT IT.

OH! YOU MUST GO TO HER AND *IMPLORE* HER. YOU MUST CALL HER YOUR *TERPSICHORE*.

YOU MUST WRITE POEMS FOR HER, MIGHTY ODES—I SHALL HELP YOU WRITE THEM—AND THUS—AND *ONLY* THUS—SHALL YOU WIN YOUR TRUE LOVE'S HEART.

I DON'T ACTUALLY NEED TO WIN HER HEART. SHE'S NOT MY TRUE LOVE. JUST SOMEONE TO TALK TO.

OF ALL THE ORGANS, THE TONGUE IS THE MOST REMARKABLE. WE UTTER WORDS BOTH SWEET AND SOUR WITH THE SAME TONGUE.

YOU *SHOULD*, SIR! YOU *MUST*!

I SHOULDN'T.

I SHALL WRITE ABOUT IT WHEN THE BATTLE'S LOST AND WON.

BUT IF I *UNFADE* FOR ONE PERSON, IT MAKES IT EASIER FOR OTHER PEOPLE TO SEE ME.

AH, LIST TO ME, YOUNG HERO, YOUNG ALEXANDER. IF YOU DARE NOTHING, THEN WHEN THE DAY IS OVER, NOTHING IS ALL YOU WILL HAVE GAINED.

GOOD POINT.

BOD WAS PLEASED WITH HIMSELF, AND GLAD HE HAD THOUGHT OF ASKING THE POET FOR ADVICE.

REALLY, IF YOU CAN'T TRUST A POET TO OFFER SENSIBLE ADVICE, WHO *CAN* YOU TRUST?

WHICH REMINDED HIM...

MISTER TROT? TELL ME ABOUT REVENGE.

DISH BEST SERVED COLD.

DO NOT TAKE REVENGE IN THE HEAT OF THE MOMENT, INSTEAD, WAIT UNTIL THE HOUR IS PROPITIOUS. THERE WAS A GRUB STREET HACK NAMED O'LEARY...

AN IRISHMAN, I SHOULD ADD....

WHO HAD THE *NERVE*, THE CONFOUNDED *CHEEK*, TO WRITE OF MY FIRST SLIM VOLUME...

A NOSEGAY of BEAUTY ASSEMBLED for GENTLEMEN of QUALITY

IT IS INFERIOR DOGGEREL OF NO WORTH WHATSOEVER, AND THE PAPER IT IS WRITTEN ON WOULD BE BETTER USED TO...

NO!

I CANNOT SAY.

LET US SIMPLY AGREE THAT IT WAS A MOST VULGAR STATEMENT.

BUT YOU GOT YOUR REVENGE ON HIM?

ON HIM AND HIS ENTIRE PESTILENT BREED. OH, I HAD MY REVENGE, MASTER OWENS, AND IT WAS A *TERRIBLE* ONE.

"I WROTE A LETTER, WHICH I NAILED TO THE DOORS OF THE PUBLIC HOUSES IN LONDON WHERE SUCH SCRIBBLING FOLK WERE WONT TO FREQUENT.

"AND I EXPLAINED THAT, GIVEN THE FRAGILITY OF THE GENIUS POETICAL, I WOULD HENCEFORTH WRITE NOT FOR THEM, BUT ONLY FOR MYSELF AND POSTERITY, AND THAT I SHOULD, AS LONG AS I LIVED, PUBLISH NO MORE POEMS...

...FOR *THEM!*

"THUS I LEFT INSTRUCTIONS THAT UPON MY DEATH, MY POEMS WERE TO BE BURIED WITH ME, AND THAT ONLY WHEN POSTERITY REALIZED MY GENIUS, ONLY THEN WAS MY COFFIN TO BE DISINTERRED AND MY POEMS REMOVED FROM MY COLD DEAD HANDS TO FINALLY BE PUBLISHED TO THE DELIGHT AND APPROBATION OF ALL.

"IT IS A TERRIBLE THING TO BE AHEAD OF YOUR TIME."

AND AFTER YOU DIED, THEY DUG YOU UP, AND THEY PRINTED THE POEMS?

NOT YET, NO. BUT THERE IS STILL PLENTY OF TIME. POSTERITY IS VAST.

SO... THAT WAS YOUR REVENGE.

INDEED. AND A MIGHTILY POWERFUL AND CUNNING ONE AT THAT.

YE-ES.

... 66 ...

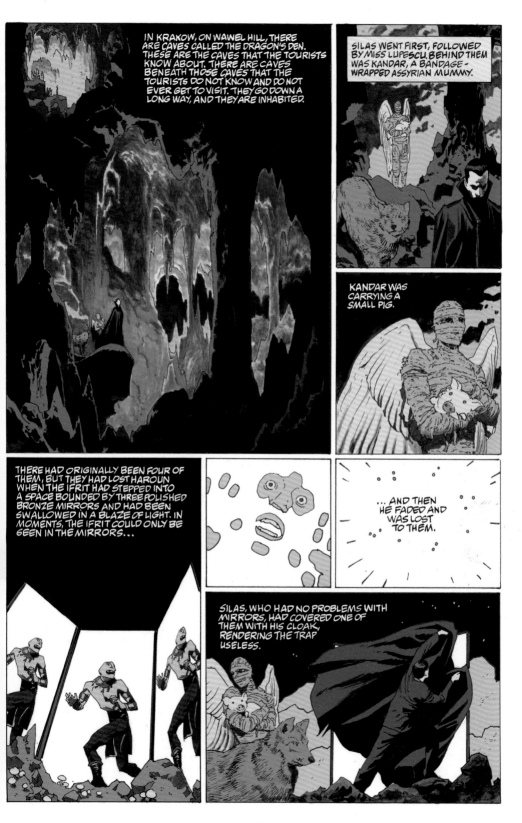

IN KRAKOW, ON WAWEL HILL, THERE ARE CAVES CALLED THE DRAGON'S DEN. THESE ARE THE CAVES THAT THE TOURISTS KNOW ABOUT. THERE ARE CAVES BENEATH THOSE CAVES THAT THE TOURISTS DO NOT KNOW AND DO NOT EVER GET TO VISIT. THEY GO DOWN A LONG WAY, AND THEY ARE INHABITED.

SILAS WENT FIRST, FOLLOWED BY MISS LUPESCU, BEHIND THEM WAS KANDAR, A BANDAGE-WRAPPED ASSYRIAN MUMMY.

KANDAR WAS CARRYING A SMALL PIG.

THERE HAD ORIGINALLY BEEN FOUR OF THEM, BUT THEY HAD LOST HAROUN WHEN THE IFRIT HAD STEPPED INTO A SPACE BOUNDED BY THREE POLISHED BRONZE MIRRORS AND HAD BEEN SWALLOWED IN A BLAZE OF LIGHT. IN MOMENTS, THE IFRIT COULD ONLY BE SEEN IN THE MIRRORS...

... AND THEN HE FADED AND WAS LOST TO THEM.

SILAS, WHO HAD NO PROBLEMS WITH MIRRORS, HAD COVERED ONE OF THEM WITH HIS CLOAK, RENDERING THE TRAP USELESS.

... 73 ...

IS IT FOR SCHOOL?

IT'S LOCAL HISTORY.

WE'VE GOT THE LOCAL PAPER ON MICROFICHE. ONE DAY, WE'LL HAVE IT ALL DIGITIZED. NOW, WHAT DATES ARE YOU AFTER?

YES?

I WANTED TO SEE SOME OLD NEWSPAPER CLIPPINGS.

ABOUT THIRTEEN OR FOURTEEN YEARS AGO. I CAN'T BE MORE SPECIFIC THAN THAT. I'LL KNOW IT WHEN I SEE IT.

COME WITH ME.

HERE.

GO WILD.

SCARLETT ASSUMED THAT THE MURDER OF A FAMILY WOULD BE FRONT PAGE NEWS BUT INSTEAD, WHEN SHE EVENTUALLY FOUND IT...

IT'S BURIED ON PAGE FIVE.

THERE WAS NO COLOR IN THE ARTICLE, NO DESCRIPTION, JUST AN UNDERSTATED LIST OF EVENTS.

ARCHITECT RONALD DORIAN, 36, HIS WIFE, CARLOTTA, 34, A PUBLISHER, AND THEIR DAUGHTER, MISTY, 7, WERE FOUND DEAD AT 33 DUNSTAN ROAD. FOUL PLAY IS SUSPECTED. A POLICE SPOKESMAN SAID THAT IT WAS TOO EARLY TO COMMENT AT THIS STAGE OF THEIR INVESTIGATIONS, BUT THAT SIGNIFICANT LEADS ARE BEING FOLLOWED.

THIS, YOUNG SCARLETT, IS WHERE WE LOCAL HISTORIANS COME INTO OUR OWN. LEAVE IT WITH ME. I'LL FIND OUT EVERYTHING I CAN AND REPORT BACK.

THANK YOU.

UM. I ASSUME THIS PHONE CALL IS BECAUSE IF NOONA THOUGHT THERE WERE MURDERS GOING ON IN MY HOME, YOU'D NEVER BE ALLOWED TO SEE ME OR THE GRAVEYARD AGAIN. SO, UM, SUPPOSE I WON'T MENTION IT UNLESS YOU DO.

SEE YOU AT SEVEN. WITH CHOCOLATES.

THANK YOU, MR. FROST!

DINNER WAS REMARKABLY PLEASANT. THE BURNT SMELL HAD GONE FROM THE KITCHEN, AND THE CHOCOLATES, WHICH THEY HAD FOR DESSERT WERE PERFECT. MR. FROST SAT AND TALKED WITH THEM UNTIL ABOUT 10 P.M., WHEN HE SAID THAT HE NEEDED TO GET HOME.

TIME, TIDE, AND HISTORICAL RESEARCH WAIT FOR NO MAN.

SCARLETT TRIED TO FIND BOD IN HER DREAMS THAT NIGHT, BUT WHEN SHE DID DREAM IT WAS OF WANDERING AROUND GLASGOW CITY CENTER WITH HER OLD FRIENDS. THEY WERE HUNTING FOR A SPECIFIC STREET, BUT ALL THEY FOUND WAS A SUCCESSION OF DEAD ENDS, ONE AFTER ANOTHER.

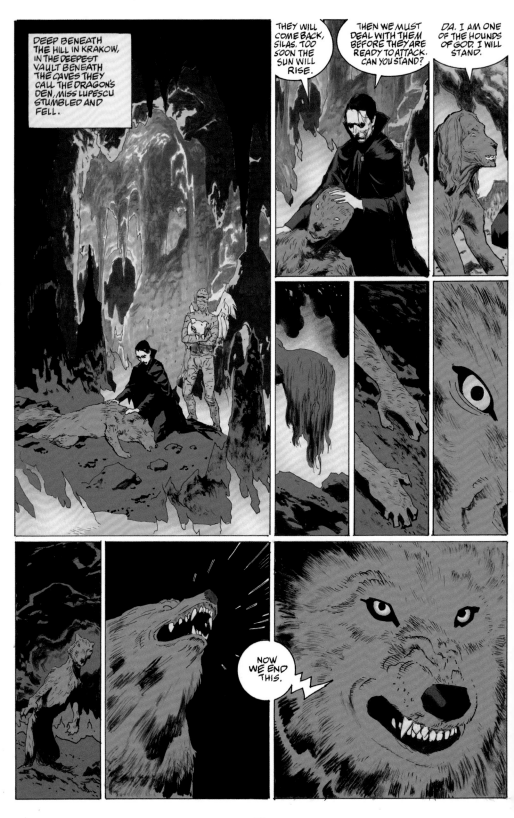

DEEP BENEATH THE HILL IN KRAKOW, IN THE DEEPEST VAULT BENEATH THE CAVES THEY CALL THE DRAGON'S DEN, MISS LUPESCU STUMBLED AND FELL.

THEY WILL COME BACK, SILAS. TOO SOON THE SUN WILL RISE.

THEN WE MUST DEAL WITH THEM BEFORE THEY ARE READY TO ATTACK. CAN YOU STAND?

DA. I AM ONE OF THE HOUNDS OF GOD. I WILL STAND.

NOW WE END THIS.

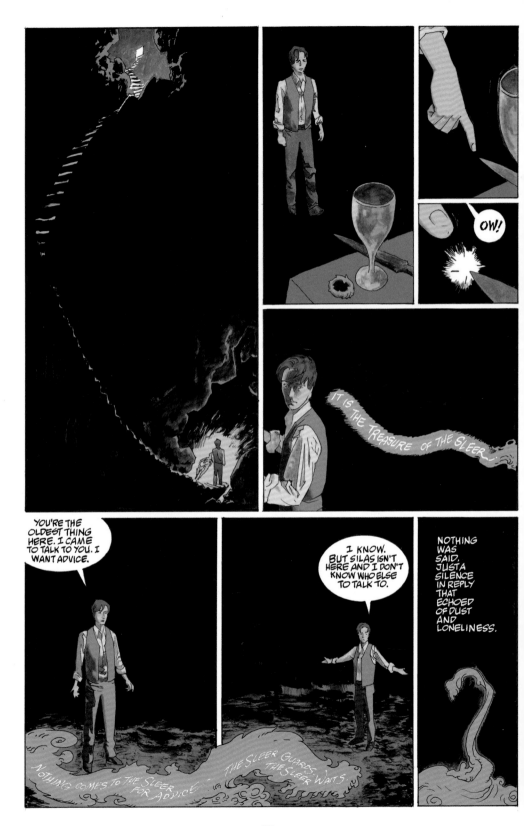

... 99 ...

WE — MY FRIENDS AND I — ARE MEMBERS OF A FRATERNAL ORGANIZATION KNOWN AS THE *JACKS OF ALL TRADES*, OR THE *KNAVES*, OR BY OTHER NAMES. WE GO BACK AN EXTREMELY LONG WAY. WE KNOW... WE *REMEMBER* THINGS THAT MOST PEOPLE HAVE *FORGOTTEN*.

THE *OLD* KNOWLEDGE.

MAGIC.

YOU KNOW A LITTLE MAGIC.

IF YOU WANT TO CALL IT THAT. BUT IT IS A VERY SPECIFIC SORT OF MAGIC. THERE'S A MAGIC YOU TAKE FROM DEATH. SOMETHING LEAVES THE WORLD, SOMETHING ELSE COMES INTO IT.

YOU KILLED MY FAMILY FOR — FOR WHAT? FOR MAGIC POWERS? THAT'S RIDICULOUS.

NO, WE KILLED YOU FOR PROTEC- TION.

" LONG TIME AGO, ONE OF OUR PEOPLE — THIS WAS BACK IN EGYPT, IN PYRAMID DAYS — HE FORESAW THAT ONE DAY, THERE WOULD BE A CHILD BORN WHO WOULD WALK THE BORDERLAND BETWEEN THE LIVING AND THE DEAD. THAT IF THIS CHILD GREW TO ADULTHOOD IT WOULD MEAN THE END OF OUR ORDER AND ALL WE STAND FOR.

" WE HAD PEOPLE CASTING NATIVITIES BEFORE LONDON WAS A VILLAGE, WE HAD YOUR FAMILY IN OUR SIGHTS BEFORE NEW AMSTERDAM BECAME NEW YORK.

" AND WE SENT WHAT WE THOUGHT WAS THE BEST AND THE SHARPEST AND THE MOST DANGEROUS OF ALL THE JACKS TO DEAL WITH YOU. TO DO IT PROPERLY, SO WE COULD TAKE ALL THE BAD JUJU AND MAKE IT WORK FOR US INSTEAD, AND KEEP EVERYTHING TICKETY-BOO FOR ANOTHER FIVE THOUSAND YEARS.

" ONLY HE DIDN'T. "

THERE'S A DESERT DOWN THERE. IF YOU LOOK FOR WATER, YOU SHOULD FIND SOME. THERE'S THINGS TO EAT IF YOU LOOK HARD, BUT DON'T ANTAGONIZE THE NIGHT-GAUNTS.

AVOID GHÛLHEIM.

THE GHOULS MIGHT WIPE YOUR MEMORIES AND MAKE YOU INTO ONE OF THEM, OR THEY MIGHT WAIT UNTIL YOU'VE ROTTED DOWN, AND THEN EAT YOU.

"EITHER WAY, YOU CAN DO BETTER."

WHY ARE YOU TELLING ME THIS?

BECAUSE OF THEM.

THERE'S NO BOD...

WHERE ARE YOU? THE DEUCE TAKE YOU! WHERE ARE YOU?

GHOUL-GATES ARE MADE TO BE OPEN AND THEN CLOSED AGAIN.

YOU CAN'T LEAVE THEM OPEN. THEY WANT TO CLOSE.

... 111 ...

WHEN SCARLETT HEARD THE CRASHING NOISE FROM ABOVE, SHE MADE HER WAY CAREFULLY DOWN THE STEPS.

SHE MADE IT TO THE BOTTOM OF THE STONE STEPS. SHE WAS SCARED: SCARED OF NICE MR. FROST AND HIS SCARIER FRIENDS; SCARED OF THIS ROOM AND ITS MEMORIES; EVEN, IF SHE WERE HONEST, A LITTLE AFRAID OF BOD. HE WAS NO LONGER A QUIET BOY WITH A MYSTERY....

HE'S SOMETHING DIFFERENT NOW, SOMETHING NOT QUITE HUMAN.

I WONDER WHAT MUM'S THINKING RIGHT NOW?

SHE'LL BE PHONING MR. FROST'S HOUSE OVER AND OVER TO FIND OUT WHEN I'M GOING TO GET BACK.

IF I GET OUT OF THIS ALIVE, I'M GOING TO FORCE HER TO GET ME A PHONE. IT'S RIDICULOUS. I'M THE ONLY PERSON IN MY YEAR WHO DOESN'T HAVE HER OWN PHONE, PRACTICALLY.

I MISS MY MUM.

SHE HAD NOT THOUGHT ANYONE HUMAN COULD MOVE THAT SILENTLY THROUGH THE DARK...

DO ANYTHING CLEVER — DO ANYTHING AT ALL — AND I WILL CUT YOUR THROAT. DO YOU UNDERSTAND?

MM-HMM.

... 120 ...

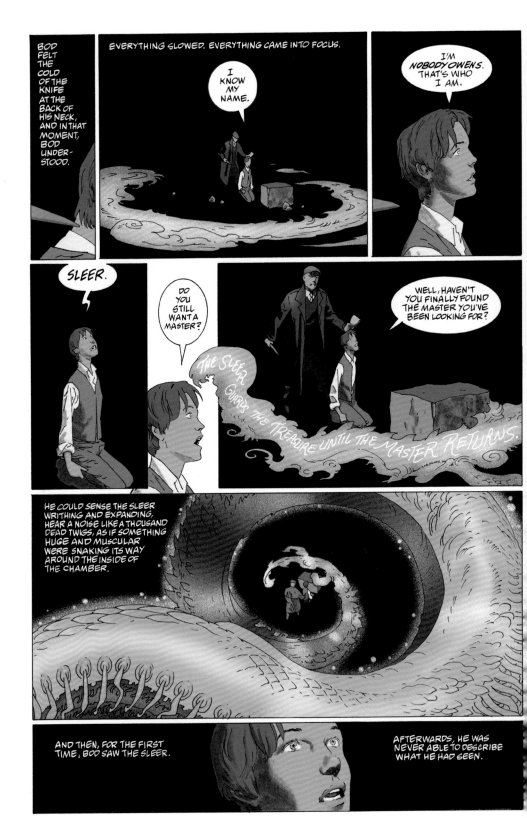

BOD FELT THE COLD OF THE KNIFE AT THE BACK OF HIS NECK, AND IN THAT MOMENT, BOD UNDERSTOOD.

EVERYTHING SLOWED. EVERYTHING CAME INTO FOCUS.

I KNOW MY NAME.

I'M *NOBODY OWENS.* THAT'S WHO I AM.

SLEER.

DO YOU STILL WANT A MASTER?

WELL, HAVEN'T YOU FINALLY FOUND THE MASTER YOU'VE BEEN LOOKING FOR?

THE SLEER GUARDS THE TREASURE UNTIL THE MASTER RETURNS.

HE COULD SENSE THE SLEER WRITHING AND EXPANDING, HEAR A NOISE LIKE A THOUSAND DEAD TWIGS, AS IF SOMETHING HUGE AND MUSCULAR WERE SNAKING ITS WAY AROUND THE INSIDE OF THE CHAMBER.

AND THEN, FOR THE FIRST TIME, BOD SAW THE SLEER.

AFTERWARDS, HE WAS NEVER ABLE TO DESCRIBE WHAT HE HAD SEEN.

THE FACES OF THE SLEER NUZZLED THE AIR ABOUT JACK TENTATIVELY, AS IF THEY WANTED TO STROKE OR CARESS HIM.

WHAT'S HAPPENING? WHAT IS IT? WHAT DOES IT DO?

IT'S CALLED THE SLEER. IT GUARDS THE PLACE. IT NEEDS A MASTER TO TELL IT WHAT TO DO.

OF COURSE. IT'S BEEN WAITING FOR ME. AND YES. OBVIOUSLY, I AM ITS NEW *MASTER!*

BEAUTIFUL.

MASTER?

MASTER

GET BACK!

KEEP AWAY FROM ME!

DON'T GET ANY CLOSER!

SCARLETT.

I WANT TO SEE. I WANT TO SEE WHAT'S HAPPENING.

WHAT SCARLETT SAW WAS NOT WHAT BOD SAW. SHE DID NOT SEE THE SLEER, AND THAT WAS A MERCY. SHE SAW THE MAN JACK, THOUGH.

HE WAS FLOATING IN THE AIR, FIVE, THEN TEN FEET ABOVE THE GROUND, SLASHING WILDLY AT THE AIR WITH TWO KNIVES, TRYING TO STAB SOMETHING SHE COULD NOT SEE, IN A DISPLAY THAT WAS OBVIOUSLY HAVING NO EFFECT.

SHE SAW THE FEAR ON HIS FACE, WHICH MADE HIM LOOK LIKE MR. FROST HAD ONCE LOOKED. IN HIS TERROR HE WAS ONCE MORE THE NICE MAN WHO HAD DRIVEN HER HOME.

MR. FROST, THE MAN JACK, WHOEVER HE WAS, WAS FORCED AWAY FROM THEM ...

... UNTIL HE WAS SPREAD-EAGLED AGAINST THE SIDE OF THE CHAMBER WALL.

… 131 …

AND WHAT ABOUT THOSE OTHER MEN? DID YOU KILL THEM, TOO?

I DIDN'T KILL ANYONE.

THEN WHERE *ARE* THEY?

ONE OF THEM'S AT THE BOTTOM OF A DEEP GRAVE. THE OTHER THREE ARE... WELL, THEY'RE A LONG WAY AWAY.

YOU DIDN'T KILL THEM?

OF COURSE NOT.

THIS IS MY HOME. WHY WOULD I WANT THEM HANGING AROUND HERE FOR THE REST OF TIME?

LOOK, IT'S OKAY. I DEALT WITH THEM.

YOU AREN'T A *PERSON.* PEOPLE DON'T *BEHAVE* LIKE YOU. YOU'RE AS BAD AS *HE* WAS. YOU'RE A MONSTER.

NO. IT WASN'T LIKE THAT.

I'M AFRAID YOU DO BOD AN INJUSTICE.

I WANT TO GO HOME. PLEASE?

BOD STARED AT SCARLETT AS SHE WALKED AWAY, HOPING THAT SHE WOULD TURN AND LOOK BACK, THAT SHE WOULD SMILE OR JUST LOOK AT HIM, WITHOUT FEAR IN HER EYES.

BUT SCARLETT DID NOT TURN.

SHE SIMPLY WALKED AWAY.

A MAN BROUGHT SCARLETT HOME.

LATER, SCARLETT'S MOTHER COULD NOT REMEMBER QUITE WHAT HE HAD TOLD HER, ALTHOUGH, DISAPPOINTINGLY, SHE HAD LEARNED...

OH, THAT *NICE* JAY FROST.

UNAVOIDABLY FORCED TO LEAVE TOWN.

THE MAN TALKED WITH THEM, IN THE KITCHEN, ABOUT THEIR LIVES AND DREAMS, AND BY THE END OF THEIR CONVERSATION, SCARLETT'S MOTHER HAD SOMEHOW *DECIDED* THEY WOULD BE RETURNING TO GLASGOW.

SCARLETT WOULD BE HAPPY TO BE NEAR HER FATHER, AND TO SEE HER OLD FRIENDS AGAIN.

NOONA EVEN PROMISED TO BUY SCARLETT A PHONE OF HER OWN.

SILAS LEFT THE GIRL AND HER MOTHER IN THE KITCHEN.

THEY BARELY REMEMBERED THAT SILAS HAD EVER BEEN THERE...

...WHICH WAS THE WAY HE LIKED IT.

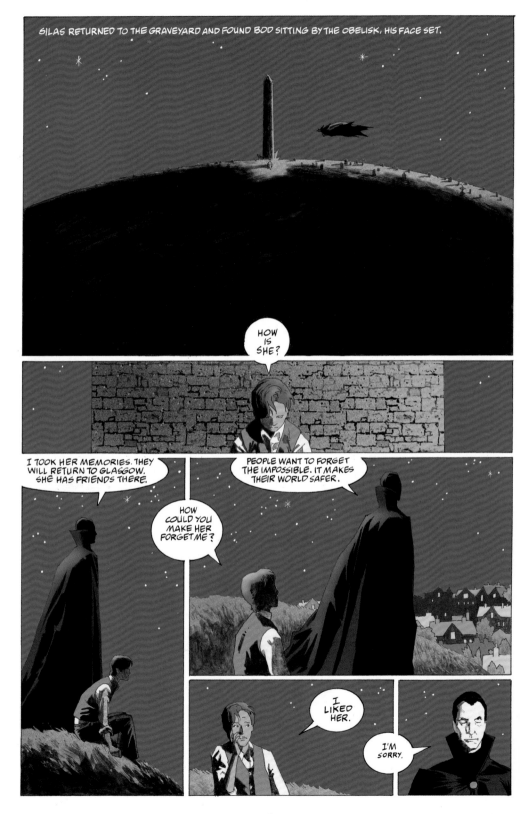

SILAS RETURNED TO THE GRAVEYARD AND FOUND BOD SITTING BY THE OBELISK, HIS FACE SET.

HOW IS SHE?

I TOOK HER MEMORIES. THEY WILL RETURN TO GLASGOW. SHE HAS FRIENDS THERE.

PEOPLE WANT TO FORGET THE IMPOSSIBLE. IT MAKES THEIR WORLD SAFER.

HOW COULD YOU MAKE HER FORGET ME?

I LIKED HER.

I'M SORRY.

BOD THOUGHT ABOUT SAYING THAT HE WASN'T HUNGRY, BUT THAT SIMPLY WAS NOT TRUE. HE FELT A LITTLE SICK AND A LITTLE LIGHT-HEADED, AND HE WAS STARVING.

PIZZA?

AS BOD WALKED, HE SAW THE INHABITANTS OF THE GRAVEYARD, BUT THEY LET THE BOY AND HIS GUARDIAN PASS AMONG THEM WITH-OUT A WORD. THEY ONLY WATCHED. BOD TRIED TO THANK THEM FOR THEIR HELP, TO CALL OUT HIS GRATITUDE...

...BUT THE DEAD SAID NOTHING.

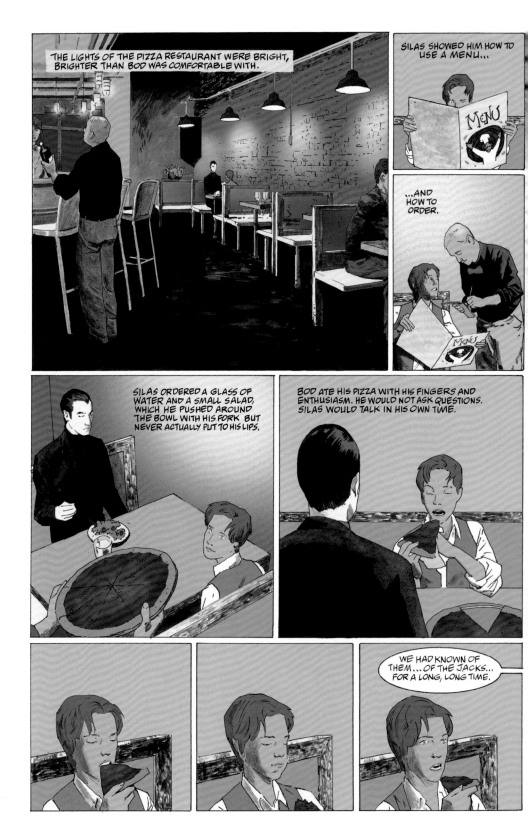

THE LIGHTS OF THE PIZZA RESTAURANT WERE BRIGHT, BRIGHTER THAN BOD WAS COMFORTABLE WITH.

SILAS SHOWED HIM HOW TO USE A MENU...

...AND HOW TO ORDER.

SILAS ORDERED A GLASS OF WATER AND A SMALL SALAD, WHICH HE PUSHED AROUND THE BOWL WITH HIS FORK BUT NEVER ACTUALLY PUT TO HIS LIPS.

BOD ATE HIS PIZZA WITH HIS FINGERS AND ENTHUSIASM. HE WOULD NOT ASK QUESTIONS. SILAS WOULD TALK IN HIS OWN TIME.

WE HAD KNOWN OF THEM... OF THE JACKS... FOR A LONG, LONG TIME.

... 141 ...

8
Leavings and Partings

Illustrated by P. Craig Russell, Kevin Nowlan, and Galen Showman

BOD HAD BEEN COMING DOWN HERE FOR SEVERAL MONTHS: ALONZO JONES HAD BEEN ALL OVER THE WORLD, AND HE TOOK GREAT PLEASURE IN TELLING BOD STORIES OF HIS TRAVELS. HE WOULD BEGIN BY SAYING...

NOTHING INTERESTING HAS EVER HAPPENED TO ME...

...AND I HAVE TOLD YOU ALL MY TALES.

EXCEPT... DID I EVER TELL YOU ABOUT...

... 146 ...

FEELING DISCOMFITED IN A WAY HE COULD NOT REMEMBER HAVING FELT BEFORE, BOD MADE HIS WAY BACK TO THE OWENSES' TOMB, AND WAS PLEASED TO SEE BOTH OF HIS PARENTS WAITING FOR HIM BESIDE IT.

WHY DO THEY STAND LIKE THAT?

ODD.

EVENING, BOD. I TRUST YOU ARE KEEPING WELL?

TOLERABLY WELL.

MISTRESS OWENS AND I SPENT OUR LIVES WISHING THAT WE HAD A CHILD. I DO NOT BELIEVE THAT WE COULD HAVE EVER HAD A BETTER YOUNG MAN THAN YOU, BOD.

WELL, YES, THANK YOU, BUT...

?

WHERE DID SHE GO?

OH, YES. AH, YOU KNOW BETSY. THERE'S THINGS, TIMES, WHEN... WELL, YOU DON'T KNOW WHAT TO SAY. YOU KNOW?

NO.

I EXPECT SILAS IS WAITING FOR YOU.

AND THEN HE WAS GONE.

... 151 ...

COME IN, BOD.

I CAN'T SEE ANYTHING. IT'S TOO DARK.

ALREADY?

IS THIS WHERE YOU SLEEP?

WHEN I AM FAR FROM MY HOUSE, YES.

ISN'T *THIS* YOUR HOME?

MY HOUSE IS A LONG, LONG WAY FROM HERE. THAT IS, IF IT'S STILL HABITABLE. THERE HAVE BEEN PROBLEMS IN MY NATIVE LAND, AND I AM FAR FROM CERTAIN WHAT I WILL FIND ON MY RETURN.

I AM SO PROUD OF YOU, MY SON.

THE MIDSUMMER SKY WAS ALREADY BEGINNING TO LIGHTEN IN THE EAST, AND THAT WAS THE WAY BOD BEGAN TO WALK.

THERE WAS A PASSPORT IN HIS BAG, MONEY IN HIS POCKET. THERE WAS A SMILE DANCING ON HIS LIPS, ALTHOUGH IT WAS A WARY SMILE, FOR THE WORLD IS A BIGGER PLACE THAN A LITTLE GRAVEYARD ON A HILL; AND THERE WOULD BE DANGERS IN IT AND MYSTERIES, NEW FRIENDS TO MAKE, OLD FRIENDS TO REDISCOVER, MISTAKES TO BE MADE AND MANY PATHS TO BE WALKED BEFORE HE WOULD, FINALLY, RETURN TO THE GRAVEYARD OR RIDE WITH THE LADY ON THE BROAD BACK OF HER GREAT GREY STALLION.

BUT BETWEEN NOW AND THEN THERE WAS *LIFE*...

The Graveyard Book

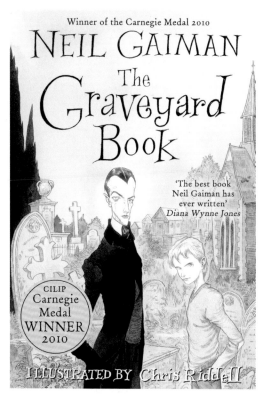

ISBN 978 0 7475 9480 2

The Carnegie and Newbery award-winning
novel from Neil Gaiman,
illustrated by Chris Riddell

Coraline

'I was enthralled. This is a marvellously strange and scary book'
Philip Pullman, Guardian

ISBN 978 1 4088 4175 4

Illustrated by Chris Riddell

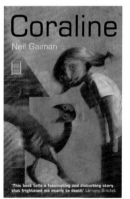

ISBN 978 0 7475 6210 8

Illustrated by
Dave McKean

ISBN 978 0 7475 9406 2

Adapted and illustrated by
P. Craig Russell

FORTUNATELY, THE MILK

'A story that is as entertaining for adults as children' *Observer*

'If you enjoy fantasy, he is irresistible' *The Times*

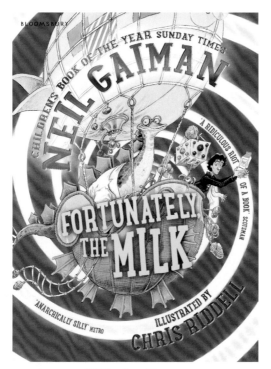

ISBN 978 1 4088 4179 2

A spectacularly silly, mind-bendingly clever, brilliantly bonkers adventure, with stunning illustrations by Chris Riddell